Jenny White

Illustrated by James Piggott

A
Surprise
for
Junior

AuthorHouse™
1663 Liberty Drive
Bloomington, IN 47403
www.authorhouse.com
Phone: 1-800-839-8640

Published by AuthorHouse 04/09/2013

ISBN: 978-1-4817-0602-5 (sc)
         978-1-4817-0603-2 (e)

authorHOUSE®

It was a beautiful fall morning and the leaves had just started to turn and fall to the ground.

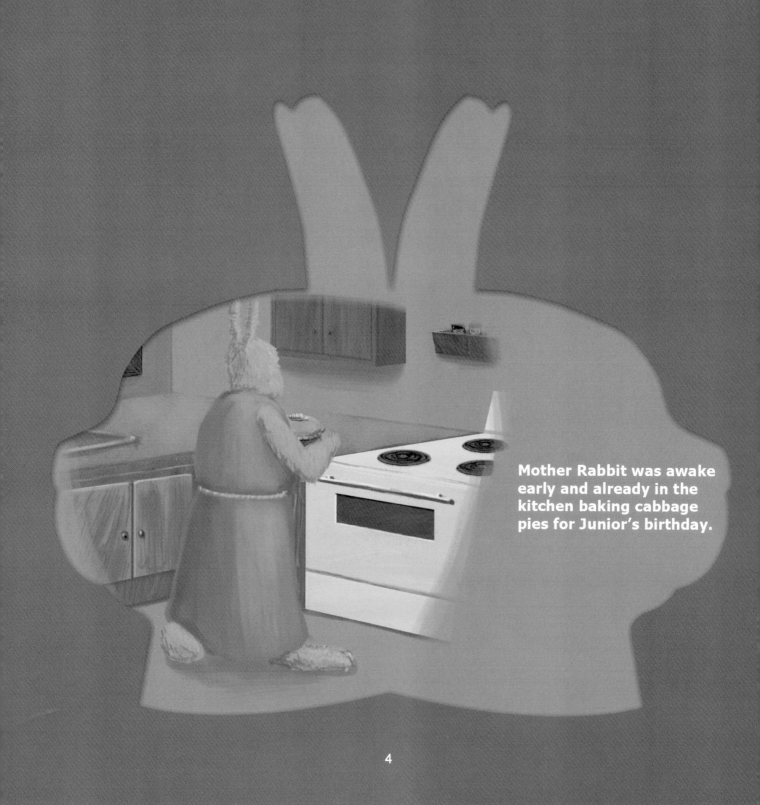

Mother Rabbit was awake early and already in the kitchen baking cabbage pies for Junior's birthday.

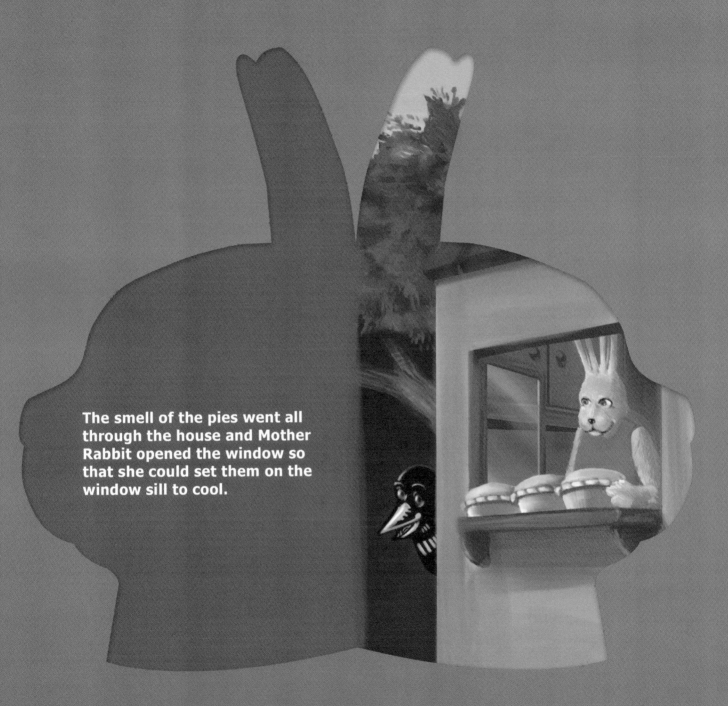

The smell of the pies went all through the house and Mother Rabbit opened the window so that she could set them on the window sill to cool.

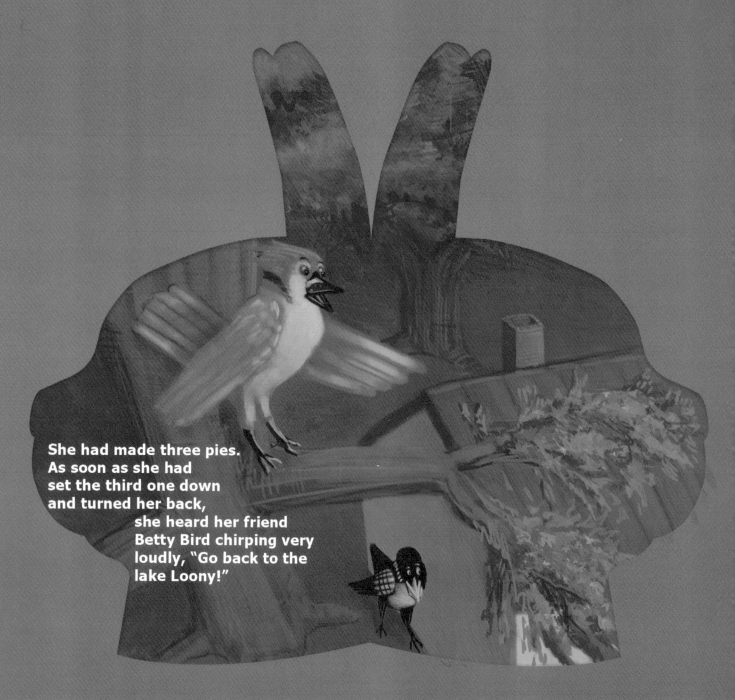

She had made three pies.
As soon as she had
set the third one down
and turned her back,
she heard her friend
Betty Bird chirping very
loudly, "Go back to the
lake Loony!"

6

Mother Rabbit turned and saw Loony Lou, the mismatching, beak-snatching, pie-napping loon flying away with one of her pies.

"Come back here with that pie!"
shouted Mother Rabbit.

"You beak-snatching,
need-a-whacking,
throw-you-in-a-sack-and-forget-
about-you pie thief!"

Papa Rabbit and Junior Rabbit, hearing all the commotion, ran into the kitchen. Mother Rabbit told them what happened.

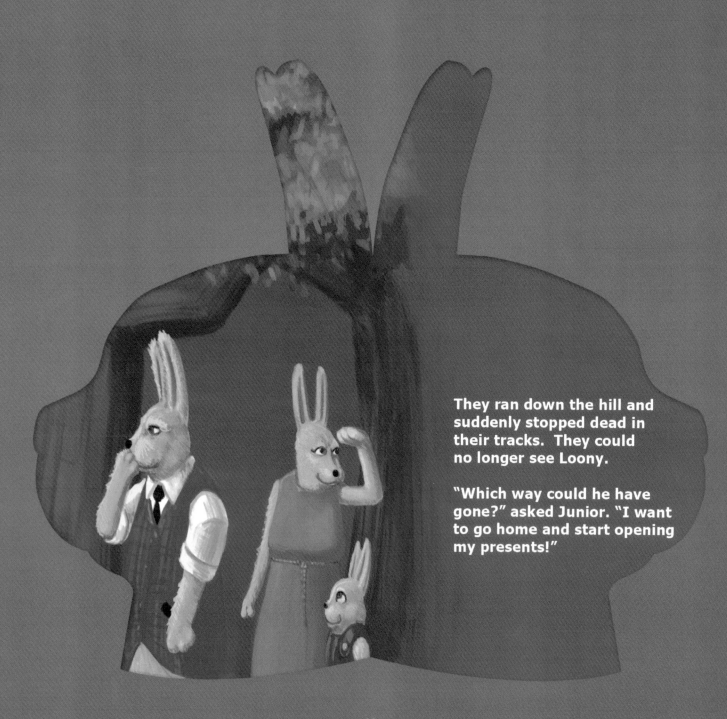

They ran down the hill and suddenly stopped dead in their tracks. They could no longer see Loony.

"Which way could he have gone?" asked Junior. "I want to go home and start opening my presents!"

"I don't know," said Papa.

"Let's ask Jenny the squirrel if she's seen him."

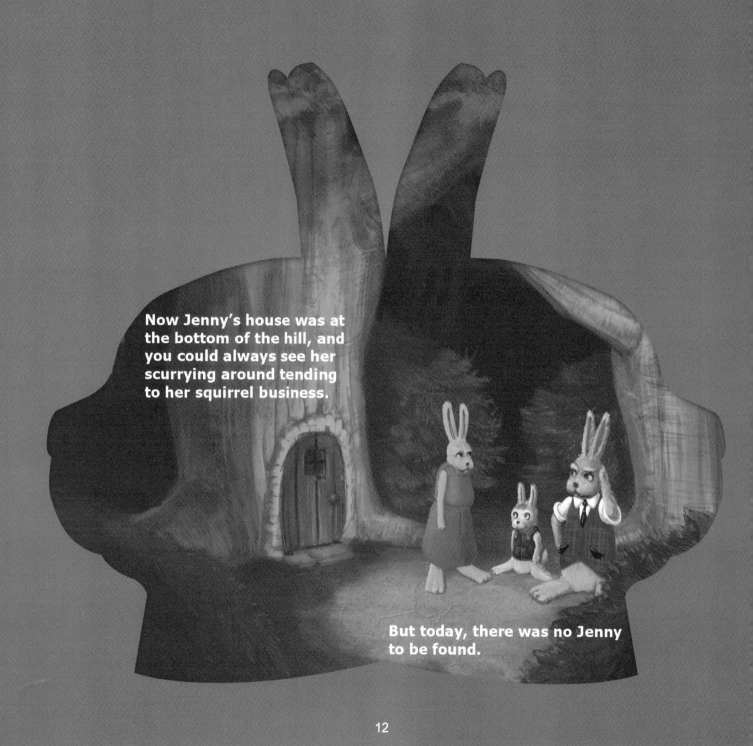

Now Jenny's house was at the bottom of the hill, and you could always see her scurrying around tending to her squirrel business.

But today, there was no Jenny to be found.

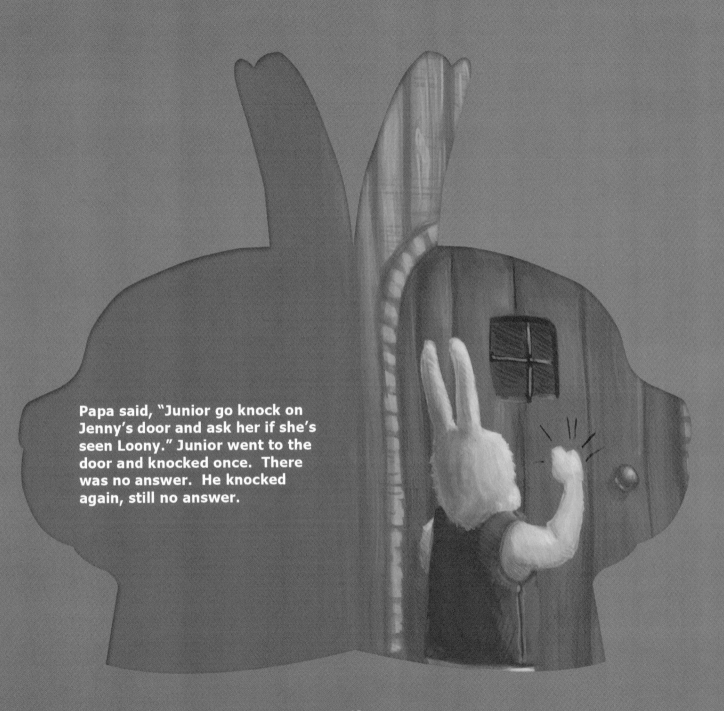

Papa said, "Junior go knock on Jenny's door and ask her if she's seen Loony." Junior went to the door and knocked once. There was no answer. He knocked again, still no answer.

"There's no one home," said Junior

Papa said, "Jenny is always home, I wonder if some-thing is wrong?"

"Let's go in and wait for her," said Papa.

"Jenny always leaves her door unlocked since that day she locked herself out of the house and Buck the cock-eyed beaver had to come and gnaw through the door so she could get in."

"It's kinda dark in here," said Papa. "Let's cut on the light."

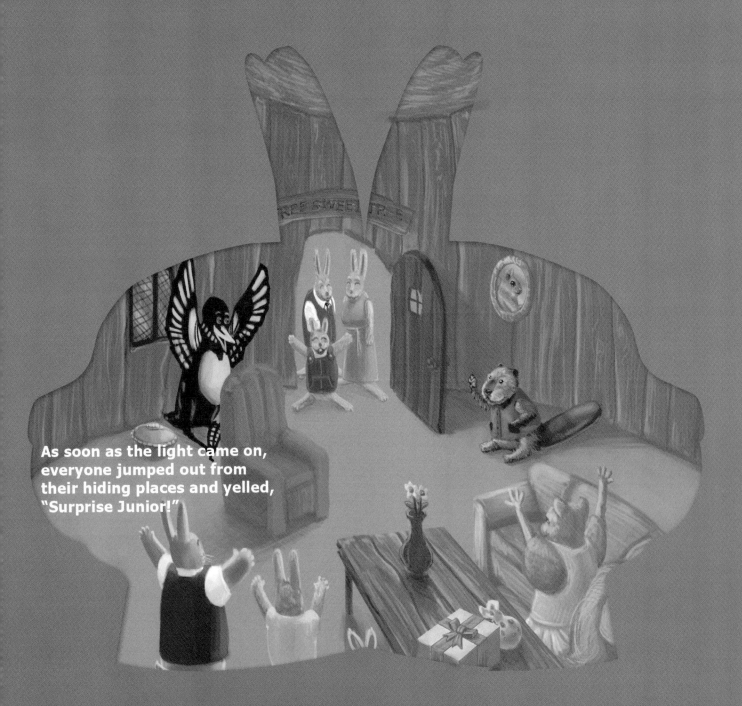

As soon as the light came on, everyone jumped out from their hiding places and yelled, "Surprise Junior!"

Junior had been fooled! He would never have thought that everything that happened had been a set-up to get him down to Jenny's house for a surprise party.

Set-up or not, Junior was so excited, he sat down in the middle of the floor and began tearing the wrapping paper off his presents!

"Come to the table everyone." Mother Rabbit said.
She stuck five candles in one of the pies and
everyone sang "Happy Birthday" to Junior.

...and, Loony the beak-snatching, mismatching, and in this case thought to be pie-napping thief, sat at the window enjoying his very own fish pie!

Jenny White is a retired educator who lives in Michigan. She is married with 4 children and 8 grandchildren. She travels frequently and volunteers at the Ronald McDonald House in MI. She is very active in her church where she teaches Sunday School, sings in the choir, is on the usher board and the Mother's board and works with the youth. She is very excited about publishing her first book, but keep looking, there's more to come.